Too much
Pinky Ponk juice!

Andrew Davenport

Once upon a time in the Night Garden...

The Tombliboos came to play.

Ombliboo, tombliboo,
knock on the door,
Ombliboo, tombliboo,
sit on the floor.
Ombliboo, tombliboo,
here is my nose,
Ombliboo, tombliboo,
that's how it goes.

One day the Tombliboos
were riding in the Pinky Ponk
with Upsy Daisy
and Igglepiggle.

Tombliboo Ooo drank up all
his Pinky Ponk juice.
Do you know what
Tombliboo Ooo did next?

Sluurrp!

That's not Tombliboo
Ooo's Pinky Ponk juice.

Sluurrp!

Neither is that!

Tombliboo Ooo drank everybody's
Pinky Ponk juice.

Wobble-grobble...

Grumble-burble-bluuurp!

Oh dear. Tombliboo Ooo has too much Pinky Ponk juice in his tummy.

Poor Tombliboo Ooo.

Wobble-grobble-grumble... burble-bluuurp!

Tombliboo Ooo went straight to bed.

Tombliboo Unn and Tombliboo Eee began to play a Tombliboo tune especially for Tombliboo Ooo.

Tiddly-plinky-plonky-onk!

Tombliboo Ooo listened.
And he began to feel better.

Tombliboo Ooo jumped out of bed
and ran all the way down
the Tombliboo stairs.

Tombliboo Ooo gave Tombliboo Unn
and Tombliboo Eee a big Tombliboo hug.

Look at that.
One, two, three happy Tombliboos.

Isn't that a pip?

Once upon a time
in the Night Garden,

Tombliboo Ooo
drank up all of
the Pinky Ponk juice.

Sluurrp!

Sluurrp!

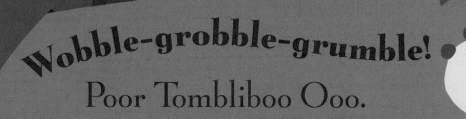

Wobble-grobble-grumble!
Poor Tombliboo Ooo.

Tombliboo music
will help!

Thank you Tombliboo Unn,
thank you Tombliboo Eee.

Time to go to sleep everybody.

Go to sleep, Tombliboos.

Go to sleep, Upsy Daisy

Go to sleep, Makka Pakka.

Go to sleep, Pontipines.

Go to sleep, Haahoos.

Go to sleep Ninky Nonk
and go to sleep, Pinky Ponk.

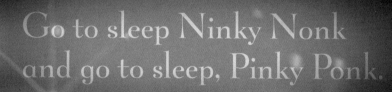

Wait a minute.
Somebody is not in bed!
Who's not in bed?
Igglepiggle is not in bed!

Don't worry, Igglepiggle...
it's time to go.